The Cosmic Climate Invention

Published and distributed by:
Voices of Future Generations International Children's Book Series
Trust for Sustainable Living
Hampstead Norreys, Berkshire, RG18 0TN, United Kingdom
Tel: +44 (0)1635 202444
Web: www.vofg.org

Special thanks to René V. Steiner for layout and graphics support:
www.steinergraphics.com.

The Voices of Future Generations International Children's Book Series:
'The Epic Eco-Inventions' by Jona David (Europe/North America), illustrated by Carol Adlam
'The Great Green Vine Invention' by Jona David (Europe/North America), illustrated by Carol Adlam
'The Tree of Hope' by Kehkashan Basu (Middle East), illustrated by Karen Webb-Meek
'The Fireflies After the Typhoon' by Anna Kuo (Asia), illustrated by Siri Vinter
'The Species-Saving Time Team' by Lautaro Real (Latin America), illustrated by Dan Ungureanu
'The Sisters' Mind Connection' by Allison Lievano-Gomez (Latin America), illustrated by Oscar Pinto
'The Forward and Backward City' by Diwa Boateng (Africa), illustrated by Meryl Treatner
'The Voice of an Island' by Lupe Vaai (Pacific Islands), illustrated by Li-Wen Chu
'The Visible Girls' by Tyronah Sioni (Pacific Islands), illustrated by Kasia Nieżywińska
'The Mechanical Chess Invention' by Jona David (Europe/North America), illustrated by Dan Ungureanu

Voices of Future Generations Children's Book Series

Under the patronage of
UNESCO

United Nations
Educational, Scientific and
Cultural Organization

CISDL
Centre for International
Sustainable Development Law

World **Future** Council

Fundación
ECOS
www.fundacion-ecos.org

unicef
MÉXICO

Trust for
Sustainable
Living

OMBUDSMAN FOR FUTURE GENERATIONS

環境品質文教基金會
Environmental Quality Protection Foundation

MOORE
CHARITABLE
FOUNDATION

This book is printed on recycled paper, using sustainable and low-carbon printing methods.

The Cosmic Climate Invention

by

jona david

Illustrations by Dan Ungureanu

foreword

I remember the exact day I met Jona. It was during high-level event on climate education and youth we co-organized with UNICEF during the Climate Week in New York in 2017. I, and everyone in the room, were particularly inspired by his energy, poise and commitment to make a difference for the Climate.

I am happy to see that in his fourth book; Jona David shows his growth as an author and also a deepened understanding of the Climate issues facing our planet and the lengths that the global community will have to go to in order to make lasting changes.

I am convinced that youth has a particularly important role to play to help us keep the Climate Issues at the front of our common agenda and spearhead the profound changes we need to see in our societies to meet the objectives of the Paris Agreement. As the IPCC, Special Report on 1.5°C informed us a few months ago: "Pathways limiting global warming to 1.5°C with no or limited overshoot would require rapid and far-reaching transitions in energy, land, urban and infrastructure (including transport and buildings), and industrial systems. These systems transitions are unprecedented in terms of scale, but not necessarily in terms of speed, and imply deep emissions reductions in all sectors, a wide portfolio of mitigation options and a significant upscaling of investments in those options."

While the Eco-Inventor Boy's inventions make a significant contribution to help reduce CO_2 and greenhouse gasses, Jona brilliantly reminds his readers that we cannot simply rely on scientists and inventions to save our earth. Every individual, including the businessman and the schoolchild, must still aspire to make changes by giving environmental issues attention in everyday life.

Just as the Eco-Inventor Boy and Little Brother inspire their schoolmates to take up their own initiatives to reduce threats to the environment, Jona's book must play an important role to awaken both adults and children around the world to our individual duty to serve our planet and simultaneously serve our communities, both local and global, in a manner that reflects ethics and equity.

— Salaheddine Mezouar,
COP 22 and CGEM President

preface

I have often paused to consider quite what it is that we should be teaching children. With climate change, arguably the greatest challenge of our time, and the need to address this as a matter of unparalleled urgency, it is perplexing that all too often we seem inert, expecting the problem to fall into someone else's hands.

"The Cosmic Climate Invention!" is a whimsical adventure with a very practical and timely message, perhaps even a timeous challenge. Although most of us may not frequent secret laboratory silos or soar in cosmic rockets, we do all have the opportunity to make a difference, to be courageous advocates for local eco-initiatives, just like the Eco-Inventor Boy and his Little Brother, and to effect positive change, not only in how we act, but also in how we interact with one another.

Jona David has dedicated his literary talents to spreading the message of how important it is to consider the health of our environment. With this, he has championed his own eco-initiatives; his constant and varied efforts inspiring other children in his community and around the world.

Perhaps it isn't about what we should be teaching children, but much more about listening to what they are already teaching us!

It gives me very great pleasure to recommend "The Cosmic Climate Invention" to all readers. Let us commit to finding solutions, making change for the better in any way we can, big or small, "cosmic" or in our own neighbourhood!

— Yvette Day,
Head of King's College School, Cambridge.

chapter 1

In a house on a lake in a very green town lived a boy and his little brother. The boy was a mad genius eco-inventor, and his joyful little brother helped to share the inventions around the world. They had many amazing adventures together.

The two boys studied in a Terribly Good School.
The Inventor Boy loved all his classes, especially maths, science and computing. Secretly, he even liked history and other subjects. But everyone knew that you're not supposed to enjoy school, so he just kept quiet when the other kids mocked academics.

The children were studying astrophysics and meteorology in their Science lessons. They were learning about climate change, and how human activity generates greenhouse gas emissions which clog up the atmosphere, changing the climate. The pupils were really worried that rising sea levels, floods, typhoons and famines could result if the problem wasn't solved in time, and if new energy sources and systems that didn't pollute were not found.

The Eco-Inventor Boy's friends were pretty different, one from the other, but they all had good ideas. One friend was fascinated by mathematics and puzzles, he was a brilliant musician and enjoyed cricket. Another friend was also an amazing musician, very strong in classics and history. A third one was a really good debater, he spoke German and was also terrific at football.

The Eco-Inventor Boy got along fine with both the music crowd, and the sports crowd, on most days. He had invented a tiny microphone bug that could project the musician's voices and instruments effortlessly. It really helped them in performances, as it was friendly, and made sure not to get in the way. He had also invented a flying quadro-copter drone with many speed and agility settings, so that sport kids could race with it, improving their skills.

But even in their Terribly Good School, there was a group of other kids who weren't really interested in anything much. They were not always very kind, pushing pupils around during games, and laughing loudly for no reason. Whenever this crowd came in, the Eco-Inventor Boy would shut down a bit. These kids felt science and other academic work was boring and useless. They didn't seem to like music, sports, drama, art or anything else much either. The academic friends didn't want to be mocked, so they kept apart.

The Eco-Inventor Boy had a new science project, something to help deal with climate change. He was able to stay away working on it, avoiding trouble most of the time. The Little Brother was a very active member of the School Eco-Society, which involved both girls and boys, and children from all the different crowds.

He loved all the different interests and couldn't understand why some friends would stay separate from each other. He could already see his own year starting to fall into separate crowds.

The Little Brother especially worried about the kids who might cause trouble. He could see that sometimes, these kids would bully others, hiding their bikes or throwing their jackets in the bins. This made him very sad.

Like the Eco-Inventor Boy, the Little Brother thought that learning things and trying to make the world a better place was brilliant. Together with his friends, he kept looking for ways to help the children who were not interested in anything.

chapter 2

After a long but exciting day of maths, science, creative writing, virtual reality programming and gargoyle maintenance, the two brothers took a train. They were visiting one of their friends who lived in the country, quite far away from their school, for the weekend.

The family's Manor House was cheerful and welcoming. The children changed into woolly jumpers and wellies and went for a long walk. They were relaxed and friendly together, and happy to get away from the sometimes difficult dynamics. The Little Brother's pet robot spider followed in the trees.

On their walk, the Little Brother spotted a very suspicious looking grain silo. It was on a path that seemed to lead back to their own town. The grain silo also had a roof that looked like it was made to open up, almost for something like a telescope.

After he got back to the Manor, the Little Brother asked his pet robot spider about the strange grain silo. Unfortunately, the spider pet had no idea either. They decided to go check it out.

At midnight, the Little Brother and his pet robot spider woke up.

His friend awoke below in the bunk bed. He wanted to come, too. They snuck outside.

When they came to the grain silo, a mysterious door had opened in the side.

When they walked through, the Little Brother and his friend found themselves on the ground floor of a fascinating tower. It was filled with an amazing particle physics laboratory.

On the circular walls, there were all kinds of charts and screens, showing real-time projections of neutrinos and other particles. A strange transparent tube ran through the room, ending in a shadowy globe with a sign reading 'Dark Matter.' A miniature Hadron Collider machine sat in the corner.

He realised immediately that this must be the location of his older brother's new climate change project! It was hidden in a grain silo, in the fields beyond their lake.

Suddenly the Little Brother heard footsteps, echoing hollowly down a steep metal spiral staircase that ran along one side of the tower.

Fortunately, it was the Eco-Inventor Boy. The children were deeply relieved. They quickly explained that they had seen the Grain Silo on their walk and had come to investigate. The older brother smiled, and then showed the children around his top-secret new project. He explained that it was both a particle physics lab (for the micro level) and an astro-physics lab (for the macro level). By joining the two with meteorology, he was hoping to solve climate change. There were some amazing inventions.

There was a Nebula Gas Fuel Cell Maker, which the Eco-Inventor Boy explained was Version 2.0, to provide sufficient power. There was also a nebula gas solidifier. In the cellar, there was a geothermal power battery, with rods stretching deep into the earth. In the middle floors, they saw special hybrid plants bred to purify air and generate oxygen from spare molecules harvested in space. There was also a completely new kind of rocket thruster, as a half-built prototype leaning against the wall.

On the top floor, the domed roof of the grain silo could be rolled back, and the children got to try out a new smart telescope which could track astrological phenomena using their gravitational waves.

1. BLUEPRINT NOTES: GEOTHERMAL POWER BATTERY

- Long silver oblong boiler shape connected to a wall of rods, full of twisting energy
- Located in cellar, as close as possible to the earth so that water can heat into steam, converted into power through turbine/current
- Tubes extending deep into the earth, for maximum heat exchange

2. BLUEPRINT NOTES: AIR-PURIFYING HYBRID PLANTS

· Silver nitrogen-based ceramic orb to hold and supply
  nutrients to the plant
· Hybrid of spider-plant and aerophyte fern
· Tiny satellite dish grafted to the centre of each
  plant, to detect gravity and sense oxygen / CO_2 levels

EYES ONL

23

3. BLUEPRINT NOTES: NEBULA GAS-POWERED ROCKET THRUSTERS

- Two long narrow rocket thruster tubes, with narrow aerodynamic shape.
- Web-like nets of new ultra-light absorbent

CONFIDENTIAL

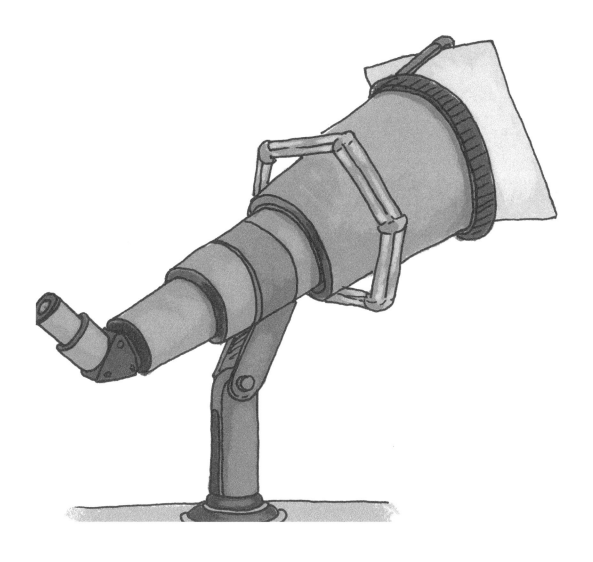

4. BLUEPRINT NOTES: SMART GRAVITATIONAL WAVES TELESCOPE

- Extended, retractable super-telescope for observing uses, pitgot aspeotdsfp
- Hexagonal ring of straight tubes containing compressed nebula gas energy, to measure gravitational waves using micro lasers tubes.
- Advanced computing system to calculate spacetime ripples.

EYES ONL

There were also several other special star spotters on the observatory deck. One wall contained a complicated scanner so the Eco-Inventor Boy could monitor, record and verify climatic changes and their impacts.

Tiny black solar power panels, built to swivel and follow the sun, were laid out like scales along the roll-back observatory dome, and were disguised as inset tiles on the sides.

"This is amazing!" said the Little Brother. "The entire grain silo has been hollowed out, and it's not just a secret laboratory. It's actually a planetarium, with its own top deck!" The Eco-Inventor Boy smiled innocently, and didn't add anything more, at least not in front of their friend.

Instead, he showed them how the whole tower was regulated by a 'smart building' system. It had a new kind of everything-proof insulation, and a display panel that showed how to control energy, heat, air and water flows, molecule movement and other aspects.

As he flipped through the displays, the Little Brother noticed something strange. All the floors of inventions took up only half the area of the silo, vertically. "There seems to be something more here" he thought, curious.

chapter 3

As they explored, the Eco-Inventor Boy explained that his whole Planetarium was actually a massive computer. Its name was Quantum, and it was friendly. Quantum was still finishing a tricky equation involving trajectories of some kind. So he sent the Little Brother and his friend down the spiral staircase, with a strict warning to turn left, not right, at the hatch.

The children made their way to the outer door, but the Little Brother's pet robot spider had his own ideas. Quick as lightning, he slipped through a hidden vent, and disappeared!

The Little Brother paused. Then, he told his friend to start walking home. "The moon is going down, and you don't see well in the dark," he said. "Don't worry about me, I'll catch up."

The Little Brother went back inside the Grain Silo Planetarium to find his pet robot spider. It was not easy to follow the echoing sounds of amazed and happy chirping as they the bounced about. He came to a strange hatch. Right or Left, Left or Right?

Eventually the Little Brother chose right, as right is always right, right? He clambered through the hatch and stepped into a large vertical brightly lit space that reached… all the way up to the Planetarium Dome!

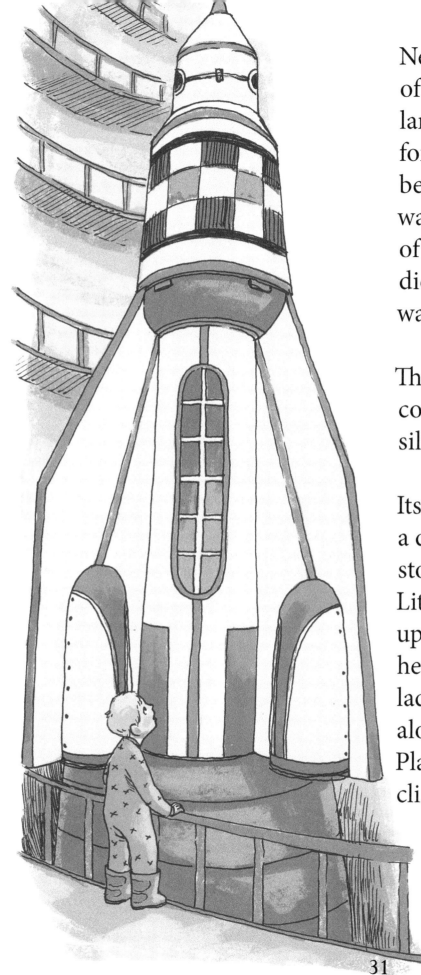

Nested inside, taking up most of the space, was something large and tall. There was a force-field which seemed to be bending the light, but since it was so big, and right in front of him, and well lit, the field didn't really disguise what he was seeing.

The Grain Silo contained a fully constructed, smooth, slender, silvery 3-story high rocket!

Its boosters reached down into a deep cellar, at least two stories below ground. The Little Brother looked up, and up, and up even further. Then, he went straight to the metal ladder that stretched upwards along the wall of the Planetarium and started climbing.

After a bit of clambering, the Little Brother reached the Observatory level where the Eco-Inventor Boy was working. "Pardon me for interrupting," he said, as his head popped out from behind the rocket's silvery nose. "But I can't help wondering… what is that 30m tall rocket doing here?"

The Eco-Inventor looked up absent-mindedly. "I built it," he answered. "Quantum and I have spotted a strange satellite near one of the moons of Mars, and it needs to be investigated. We have invented a new kind of rocket that is powered by Nebula Gas and gravitational waves instead of fossil fuels. Gravitational waves have just been discovered. They cross the universe, bending space and time."

"Our rocket doesn't generate carbon emissions that would cause climate change. If it works, we could replace the engines on all the world's jet planes and make spaceflight easier too. We're going to test it out, tonight."

"I see," exclaimed his Little Brother. "This Planetarium inside a Grain Silo are actually just a clever disguise, to hide Quantum - your super-computer and your cosmic rocket invention!" "Yes," replied the Eco-Inventor Boy. While they were chatting, the Little Brothers pet robot spider perked up, then chirped firmly to Quantum, and disappeared around the rocket. After warning how dangerous it would be, the Eco-Inventor agreed they could help with the test.

chapter 4

Soon enough, the Little Brother was at the viewing platform, gazing toward the stars. He kept an eye on the energy control panel, which operated the gravitational wave drive. The mad genius Eco-Inventor Boy was at the steering wheel, setting them on course using the trajectory holograms projected by Quantum. They would have to be super-careful, as the ozone layer was still a bit damaged, and there was a lot of debris to avoid, from old satellites.

The entrance bridge folded away, the Observatory Dome Roof rolled back, and the docking station detached. The boys were a bit unsure where their pet Robot Spider had gone. But they were distracted when they heard Quantum's soft but somehow excited voice: "Three, two, one… we have Lift-Off!

The rocket was surprisingly soundless. They slipped past the treetops. The Little Brother waved hard when he saw his friend walking below, but the force field bent the moonlight away from the rocket, and his friend couldn't see them.

They rose through the troposphere, the stratosphere, the mesosphere, then the thermosphere, and out into the exosphere. After a few moments of extreme pressure, the brothers felt themselves start to float weightlessly. Fortunately, they were both safely strapped into their booster-seats.

Soon, the main thrusters activated. The rocket zoomed into a position near Mars. Quantum was purring happily. The Earth was glowing against the horizon – an emerald green, blue and swirly white sphere. "This is amazing!" shouted the Little Brother!

"Yes," answered the Eco-Inventor Boy, "but look carefully. Can you see the places where coastlines have changed due to floods and sea level rise, where the forest is burning due to heatwaves, and where fields are turning into new deserts due to drought? This kind of loss and damage is why we need to stop climate change, before it is too late."

The children's rocket rounded Demos, one of the moons of Mars. Soon, they spotted an odd looking, spherical satellite with lots of little craters and a spiral reverse question mark on the side. They remembered it from somewhere. On the far side of the suspicious satellite, they spotted the foundations of a massive laser, with a target beam facing right towards Earth. The Little Brother didn't like that at all. "That symbol belongs to the Evil Genius, the one who cannot spell properly!" he cried.

"Yes, it must be one of his secret hide-outs." the Eco-Inventor Boy deduced. "But what is he plotting with that huge laser? It's almost like he's using it to heat up the Earth…" he added. "If its radiation is added to all the man-made CO2, methane and other gases that our old industries and waste agricultural practices are creating, and to all the deforestation, our Earth will get 4 degrees hotter, in no time at all! It could overtake all planetary threshholds, and cause major climate chaos!"

Their pet robot spider chirped loudly in alarm. "If that happens, lots of people and animals could get hurt!" cried the Little Brother. "We've got to stop him!"

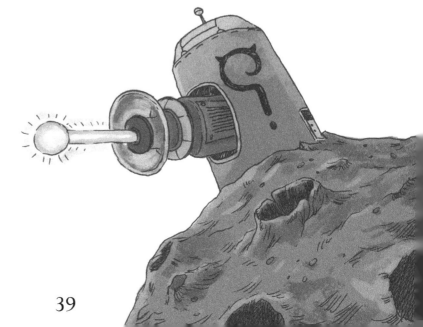

chapter 5

The Eco-Inventor Boy steered their rocket close to the fake asteroid, and its laser. He was looking for the power source. Soon, the boys spotted a globe filled with swirling glowing purple light. It was suspended just below the main controls.

"That is our missing Nebula gas fuel cell!" exclaimed the Little Brother. "Definitely," answered the Eco-Inventor Boy. "This must have been the place that the Evil Genius took our fuel cell when he stole it from us!"

The purple nebula gas globe light still glowed very warm and strong, but they could see that its energy was being sucked away by the huge laser. "This is terrible!" said the Eco-Inventor Boy.

"If he is able to finishing powering up that laser, he could fire it all the way to Earth. The increase in climate change will end civilization!" The Little Brother agreed. "That would hurt all the people and animals on our planet!"

As they swooped in for a closer look, the Little Brother's pet Robot Spider slipped out from the Nebula Gas collection ring, on the outside of the rocket, where he had been hiding the whole time. Robots don't need to breathe in space!

He leaped out and landed on the surface of the asteroid. Then, the Robot Spider swung his super-strong web across the gap, grabbing onto the Nebula Gas fuel cell, and pulling it free! Unfortunately, the asteroid hideout of the Evil Genius had not been left unprotected. Bright flashing lights shone on to their rocket, and a large Space Arm with claws sprang out, trying to grab their rocket!

The Eco-Inventor Boy steered quickly backwards, trying to pull them all safely out of harm's way.

The evil grasping Space Arm had not calculated its trajectories correctly. As it clawed towards the boys and their brave little Robot Spider, who was still holding tightly to the rescued fuel cell, it accidentally knocked into some space debris instead.

The debris crashed into the giant laser, knocking it off the fake asteroid. The broken laser turned into a tiny comet, flaring as it hurled toward Mars. It crashed, creating another crater on the red planet.

"I will need to return to tidy that up later," said the Eco-Inventor Boy responsibly. "But first, we need to help stop climate change, and get you both safely home!"

The Cosmic Climate Invention

Published and distributed by:
Voices of Future Generations International Children's Book Series
Trust for Sustainable Living
Hampstead Norreys, Berkshire, RG18 0TN, United Kingdom
Tel: +44 (0)1635 202444
Web: www.vofg.org

Special thanks to René V. Steiner for layout and graphics support:
www.steinergraphics.com.

The Voices of Future Generations International Children's Book Series:
'The Epic Eco-Inventions' by Jona David (Europe/North America), illustrated by Carol Adlam
'The Great Green Vine Invention' by Jona David (Europe/North America), illustrated by Carol Adlam
'The Tree of Hope' by Kehkashan Basu (Middle East), illustrated by Karen Webb-Meek
'The Fireflies After the Typhoon' by Anna Kuo (Asia), illustrated by Siri Vinter
'The Species-Saving Time Team' by Lautaro Real (Latin America), illustrated by Dan Ungureanu
'The Sisters' Mind Connection' by Allison Lievano-Gomez (Latin America), illustrated by Oscar Pinto
'The Forward and Backward City' by Diwa Boateng (Africa), illustrated by Meryl Treatner
'The Voice of an Island' by Lupe Vaai (Pacific Islands), illustrated by Li-Wen Chu
'The Visible Girls' by Tyronah Sioni (Pacific Islands), illustrated by Kasia Nieżywińska
'The Mechanical Chess Invention' by Jona David (Europe/North America), illustrated by Dan Ungureanu

Under the patronage of
UNESCO

United Nations
Educational, Scientific and
Cultural Organization

This book is printed on recycled paper, using sustainable and low-carbon printing methods.

He drew the rocket close to the remains of the fake asteroid, and quickly set up an invention that he'd brought with him. The Cosmic Climate Invention created a force field, a big version of the protective one in his own lab, which would help to release CO_2 and other greenhouse gases harmlessly into space. "My climate invention works to release pressure on our Earth's atmosphere, using force fields to reduce risk of additional pollution," he stated.

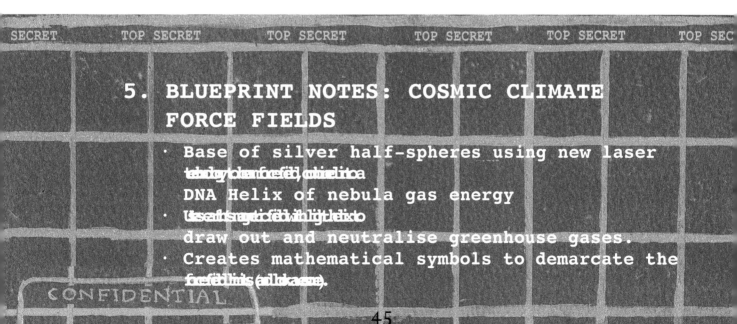

5. BLUEPRINT NOTES: COSMIC CLIMATE FORCE FIELDS

- Base of silver half-spheres using new laser ~~technology can a force field, outline into a~~
  DNA Helix of nebula gas energy
- ~~Uses a magnetic field in light helix to~~
  draw out and neutralise greenhouse gases.
- Creates mathematical symbols to demarcate the ~~force limits (all cases).~~

"This isn't a total solution," he explained. "People on Earth still need to change their habits. We need to make all our cities, industries and other constructions completely carbon neutral. Also, we should use only renewable energy sources like wind, solar, hydro, and geothermal power."

"Yes!" agreed his Little Brother. "And when we get home, we should also plant billions of trees!" The boys knew that trees absorb CO_2, an important greenhouse gas, and turn it into oxygen that humans need to breathe. Trees also help with adaptation to climate change impacts, by slowing down storms and hurricanes, by preventing floods, and by stopping soil erosion.

"Trees provide safe, natural and healthy habitats for many insects, birds and animal species. With so many animal species being hurt by the climate change that has already happened," said the Little Brother, "it is important to help them as much as we can!"

The brothers and their pet Robot Spider quickly finished their installation and turned their rocket towards their home on Earth. As their rocket powered back towards their Grain Silo, which was really a Planetarium, which was secretly a Rocket Station, they looked out over the landscape. Far below, they noticed that a new wetland was being restored by children. Their rocket landed safely, and they climbed out, happy to breathe the fresh, green air of the fens.

Soon, they were on their way back to their friend's place. As they walked through the misty sunshine, they stopped to take a closer look at the amazing green wetland restoration site. It turned out to be a new project of their Terribly Good School. The project was being done by the difficult kids! The pupils who were not usually interested in anything – not academics, sports, art, drama, nor music – were finally involved in something.

Somehow, when the whole school had become involved in a new science project, they all learned how important their own local efforts can be to fight climate change. The uninterested pupils were motivated too. They learned to be leaders, not losers. They were now hard-working members of the school's new Eco-Society. They'd been having fun building a pond, with reeds and coloured stones, to protect and enhance habitat for dragonflies and damselflies.

The Eco-Inventor Boy's friend had volunteered an area of his family's lands for one of the new dragonfly habitats. "After I saw your cosmic super-secret silo," he said, "I realised that it was the least I could do." The once-lost wetland was already nearly restored!

The Eco-Inventor Boy and his Little Brother were overjoyed. "This kind of local action right here on the ground is just as important as anything we can do from space," the Little Brother whispered to his pet Robot Spider. Everyone was happier to be making a difference. They were actually helping to take action on climate change.

Together, they could save their beautiful green and blue planet.

The End (for now)

about the author

Jona David is a 12-year-old pupil at Kings College School, Cambridge in the UK. A citizen of the UK, Canada, Switzerland and Germany, he was a Child Delegate in the 2012 United Nations (UN) Conference on Sustainable Development in Rio de Janiero, where he learned about global sustainability problems, and vowed to help make a difference. But tests revealed dyslexia, a serious learning disability, so Jona spent years memorizing spelling patterns and learning to write. At 8 years old, his eco-inventor tale was chosen for the UN Voices of Future Generations Children's Books Series. Since then, as gold-award-winning Child Author for Europe and North America, Jona has published four books and several articles. He has travelled to many countries to speak about children's rights, literacy and the environment. He co-hosted a UN Children's Summit in New York, becoming a UN Child Ambassador for global Sustainable Development Goals. He has won medals in the Trust for Sustainable Living's International Sustainability Essay Competition and Schools Debates and also awards for maths, science and the UK Model UN Debates. A founding member of the Kings Eco-Society, chess club captain, and member of his School Council, Jona enjoys science, especially astro-physics and chemistry, also maths, chess, reading, canoeing, swimming and polo. He thanks his mother, his father and his little brother Nico for all their help and inspiration.

about
the
illustrator

Dan Ungureanu has always loved drawing. As he preferred colour pencils to any toy in his early childhood, his parents decided to arrange painting lessons for him, so before learning to read he was taught to draw.

He studied painting in Romania and started working in different artistic fields, such as graphic design, concept art, story-boarding for animation movies, and painting. In 2010, he had the chance to illustrate a poem book for children and realized that this is the main path that he wants to follow. A couple of other book projects have reached his desk since then, and with each project he has learned something new.

In 2013, he decided to join the MA in Children's Book Illustration at the Cambridge School of Art, feeling the need to understand and learn more about the subject. He says this was one of his best decisions and that his main achievement in course work was gaining the confidence to not just illustrate but also write his own stories for children.

Voices of Future Generations Children's Book Series

Under the patronage of
UNESCO

United Nations
Educational, Scientific and
Cultural Organization

The United Nations Convention on the Rights of the Child

All children are holders of important human rights. Twenty-five years ago in 1989, over a hundred countries agreed on the UN Convention on the Rights of the Child. In the most important human rights treaty in history, they promised to protect and promote all children's equal rights, which are connected and equally important.

In the 54 Articles of the Convention, countries make solemn promises to defend children's needs and dreams. They recognize the role of children in realizing their rights, which requires that children be heard and involved in decision-making. In particular, Article 24 and Article 27 defend children's rights to safe drinking water, good food, a clean and safe environment, health, and quality of life. Article 29 recognizes children's rights to education that develops personality, talents and potential, respecting human rights and the natural environment.

— Dr. Alexandra Wandel
World Future Council

Voices of Future Generations Children's Book Series

United Nations
Educational, Scientific and
Cultural Organization

Under the patronage of
UNESCO

The UN Sustainable Development Goals

At the United Nations Rio+20 Conference on Sustainable Development in 2012, governments and people came together to find pathways for a safer, more fair, and greener world for all. Everyone agreed to take new action to end poverty, stop environmental problems, and build bridges to a more just future. In 283 paragraphs of *The Future We Want* Declaration, countries committed to defend human rights, steward resources, fight climate change and pollution, protect animals, plants and biodiversity, and look after oceans, mountains, wetlands and other special places.

In the United Nations, countries are committing to 17 new Sustainable Development Goals for the whole world, with targets for real actions on the ground. Clubs, governments, firms, schools and children have started over a thousand partnerships, and mobilized billions, to deliver. The future we want exists in the hearts and minds of our generation, and in the hands of us all.

— *Vuyelwa Kuuya*
Centre for International Sustainable Development Law (CISDL)

Voices of Future Generations Children's Book Series

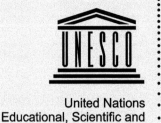

Under the patronage of
UNESCO

United Nations
Educational, Scientific and
Cultural Organization

Thanks and Inspiring Resources

'Voices of Future Generations' International Commission
Warmest thanks to the International Commission, launched in 2014 by His Excellency Judge CG Weeramantry, UNESCO Peace Education Research Award Laureate, which supports, guides and profiles this new series of Children's Books Series, including Ms Alexandra Wandel (WFC), Dr Marie-Claire Cordonier Segger (CISDL), Dr Kristiann Allen (New Zealand), Ms Irina Bokova (UNESCO), Mr Karl Hansen (Trust for Sustainable Living), Ms Emma Hopkin (UK), Dr Ying-Shih Hsieh (EQPF), Dr Maria Leichner-Reynal (Uruguay), Ms Melinda Manuel (PNG), Ms Julia Marton-Lefevre (IUCN), Dr James Moody (Australia), Ms Anna Oposa (The Philippines), Professor Kirsten Sandberg (UN CRC Chair), Ms Patricia Chaves (UN DSD), Dr Marcel Szabo (Hungary), Dr Christina Voigt (Norway), Ms Gabrielle Sacconaghi-Bacon (Moore Foundation), Ms Marcela Orvañanos de Rovzar (UNICEF Mexico) and others.

The World Future Council consists of 50 eminent global changemakers from across the globe. Together, they work to pass on a healthy planet and just societies to our children and grandchildren. (www. worldfuturecouncil.org)

United Nations Education, Science and Culture Organization (UNESCO) which celebrates its 70th Anniversary throughout 2015, strives to build networks among nations that enable humanity's moral and intellectual solidarity by mobilizing for education, building intercultural understanding, pursuing scientific cooperation, and protecting freedom of expression. (en.unesco.org)

The **United Nations Committee on the Rights of the Child (CRC)** is the body of 18 independent experts that monitors implementation of the Convention on the Rights of the Child, and its three Optional Protocols, by its State parties. (www.ohchr.org)

United Nations Environment Programme (UNEP) provides leadership and encourages partnership in caring for the environment by inspiring, informing, and enabling nations and peoples to improve their quality of life without compromising that of future generations. (www.unep.org)

International Union for the Conservation of Nature (IUCN) envisions a just world that values and conserves nature, working to conserve the integrity and diversity of nature and to ensure that any use of natural resources is equitable and ecologically sustainable. (www.iucn.org)

Centre for International Sustainable Development Law (CISDL) supports understanding, development and implementation of law for sustainable development by leading legal research through scholarship and dialogue, and facilitating legal education through teaching and capacity-building. (www.cisdl.org)

Trust for Sustainable Living and its Living Rainforest Centre exist to further the understanding of sustainable living in the United Kingdom and abroad through high-quality education. (www. livingrainforest.org)

Environmental Quality Protection Foundation (EQPF) established in 1984 is the premier ENGO in Taiwan. Implementing environmental education, tree plantation, and international participation through coordinating transdisciplinarity resources to push forward environmental and sustainable development in our time.

Voices of Future Generations Children's Book Series

About the 'Voices of Future Generations' Series

To celebrate the 25th Anniversary of the United Nations Convention on the Rights of the Child, the Voices of Future Generations Children's Book Series, led by the United Nations and a consortium of educational charities including the World Future Council (WFC), the Centre for International Sustainable Development Law (CISDL), the Environmental Quality Protection Foundation (EQPF), the Fundacion Ecos and the Trust for Sustainable Living (TSL) among others, also the Future Generations Commissioners of several countries, and international leaders from the UN Division for Sustainable Development, the UN Committee on the Rights of the Child, the UN Education, Science and Culture Organisation (UNESCO), the International Union for the Conservation of Nature (IUCN), and other international organizations, has launched the new Voices of Future Generations Series of Children's Books.

Every year we feature stories from our selected group of child authors, inspired by the outcomes of the Earth Summit, the Rio+20 United Nations Conference on Sustainable Development (UNCSD) and the world's Sustainable Development Goals, and by the Convention on the Rights of the Child (CRC) itself. Our junior authors, ages 8-12, are concerned about future justice, poverty, the global environment, education and children's rights. Accompanied by illustrations, each book profiles creative, interesting and adventurous ideas for creating a just and greener future, in the context of children's interests and lives.

We aim to publish the books internationally in ten languages, raising the voices of future generations and spread their messages for a fair and sustainable tomorrow among their peers and adults, worldwide. We welcome you to join us in support of this inspiring partnership, at www.vofg.org.